BLUE-RiBBON BLUES

Read all the books about Barkley's School for Dogs!

BLUE-RIBBON BLUES

By Marcia Thornton Jones and Debbie Dadey

Illustrated by Amy Wummer

SCHOLASTIC INC.

New York Toronto London Auckland Sydney
Mexico City New Delhi Hong Kong Buenos Aires

To Mariel, Ian, and Julia Abbene, great
neighbors   —DD

To Judy Minnehan, Lewana Sexton, Lee
Bamberger, and Ed Amend—four blue-ribbon
friends!   —MTJ

ISBN 0-439-42950-1

12 11 10 9 8 7 6 5 4 3   7/0

Printed in the U.S.A.   40

First Scholastic printing, October 2002

Book design by Dawn Adelman

This book is set in 14-point Cheltenham.

Contents

DOG TROUBLE

"Slow down, Jack," Maggie called.

Of course, I heard her. After all, I consider myself something of a Wonder Dog. Jack, the Wonder Dog, to be precise. My ears can pick up the sound of a toy squeaking a block away, but the morning was too perfect for walking slowly. I tugged harder at my leash, hoping Maggie would speed up.

"Careful, you might run into someone," Maggie warned.

I've run into people before. It's not my

idea of a good time, believe me. But now, I know just what to do. Whenever I see shoes in my Wonder Dog view, I bark. It never fails. Whoever is in those shoes jumps out of my way faster than a flea on a pancake griddle.

I turned a corner. Pink slippers popped into view. Naturally, I barked, only these shoes didn't jump out of the way.

"AAAHHHYYYEEEE!" the person in them screamed. It was no little scream, either. This scream was loud enough to bring every dog within a hundred miles to a screeching halt.

I looked up into the face of a human. I knew this human. Miss Frimple.

Miss Frimple lived across the hall from us with her sassy cat, Tazz. I had helped Tazz out of a scrape or two in the past— and I hate to admit, she's helped me a few times. Tazz wasn't bad, as far as cats go, but as long as I had known Miss Frimple, she had never smiled at me. Not once. Today was no exception.

"That dog almost gave me a heart attack," Miss Frimple told Maggie. "He should not be allowed to bark at everyone he passes on the street."

There was something about Miss Frimple that made my Wonder Dog nose itch. That's why I sneezed. Unfortunately, I sneezed near her shoes.

"Get that animal away from me," Miss

Frimple snapped, finally moving her pink slippers away from my nose.

"Jack didn't mean to sneeze on you," Maggie said in a very polite voice. "Maybe he's allergic to fuzzy slippers." She giggled.

Miss Frimple did not laugh. Maggie's smile quickly turned upside down. I didn't blame her. Miss Frimple could put ·a frown on anyone's face.

I never like it when Maggie is unhappy, and this time, it was all Miss Frimple's fault. I let out a little growl to let Miss Frimple know I didn't approve.

"Now that dog is growling at me!" Miss Frimple screamed.

"I'm sorry," Maggie said. "It will never happen again."

"We'll see about that," Miss Frimple said as she hurried away.

Maggie got down on her knees and hugged my neck. There's nothing that can

compare to a hug from a dog's human. Nothing. I snuggled my nose into her hair.

"Oh, Jack." Maggie's voice caught in her throat when she said it. "It makes me sad when Miss Frimple is mean."

Her words hurt worse than a hundred bee stings. A Wonder Dog should always make sure his human is happy. It was up to me to make her smile again.

I licked Maggie's fingers and wagged my tail, but she still wasn't smiling when she left me at Barkley's School for Dogs.

DOG-AWESOME NEWS

Maggie was sad, and I felt dog-awful. I was sure my friends would know what to do. I rushed into the Barkley's School for Dogs play yard. My friends were there, all right, but not a single one of them noticed I had arrived.

Floyd, the beagle, was throwing a rubber ducky up in the air.

Blondie, the most beautiful poodle in the world, was busy fluffing out her tail.

Bubba, the pup, ran in circles.

Casanova, the Chihuahua, hopped up

and down in front of Rhett and Scarlett, two Irish setters.

Not a single one of them noticed my droopy tail.

I looked for Woodrow. Woodrow, a basset hound, was the wisest dog in the yard. He would be able to help me. Woodrow was there, but he was doing what he did best. Sleeping.

Petey, the new dog in town, was nearby. "Hey!" I yelped. "What's all the excitement about?"

The little white-and-brown terrier didn't hear me. He had his head stuck down in a hole. He always had his head down in a hole because he spent most of his days digging.

I walked up to Petey. "What's going on?" I asked.

But Petey bounded away before I could finish my question. A pile of dirt had caught his attention. He dived at the dirt and started digging. That was just like Petey. He loved to dig more than anything.

Not a single hound was willing to tell me what was going on, and I didn't like it. There was only one thing to do. Howl.

I sat my tail down and lifted my chin to the sky. Then I let out a note so loud I was sure that windows rattled in the apartment building three blocks away.

"Quit that racket," Woodrow said from his napping place.

"Finally," I said, "a dog who can tell me what is going on around here."

"I'll tell you," Woodrow said before yawning. "The rest of the pack is a bit excited over the news."

"What news?" I asked.

"The Open House and Agility Contest," Woodrow continued. "Everyone's owner will be here to see the contest. It's our day to show off what we've learned at school. The winner gets a blue ribbon."

"A contest?" I yelped. "With ribbons? That's dog-awesome!"

"Yep," Woodrow said with another yawn. "All this excitement over a reward made of cloth."

"Not just any cloth—" I whispered, "a blue ribbon!"

I closed my eyes and imagined Fred Barkley, the school's owner, pinning a giant blue ribbon to my collar. Maggie would be there, hanging on to my leash, a

smile on her face. She would be proud, realizing what a Wonder Dog I really was. We'd parade down the sidewalk, through the park, all the way home. People would stop and stare. Even Miss Frimple and her furry cat would be dazzled.

"I'm going to win that ribbon," I said out loud. "I'm going to make Maggie proud and happy again!"

Woodrow sighed. "Your daydream might just have another ending. I know a different dog that's determined to win," he said. "Sweetcakes."

DOG'S WORST NIGHTMARE

As if she had heard Woodrow say her name, Sweetcakes marched to the middle of the yard.

Sweetcakes was the biggest Doberman pinscher in town. It's true, most Dobermans are nice and smart. But just because Sweetcakes's human owned Barkley's School for Dogs, she acted like everyone's boss.

The yard at Barkley's School for Dogs was a full-fledged agility course: full of tunnels to run through, seesaws to balance on, and bars to jump over. If it weren't for Sweetcakes, it would be a fun place to spend a day.

"Listen up," Sweetcakes barked.

"Listen, listen," Clyde repeated. Not only did the little bulldog follow Sweetcakes everywhere, he also echoed whatever she said. Today was no different.

"You all heard about the grand agility competition," Sweetcakes howled, "but

get this through those floppy ears of yours. You might as well not bother dragging your humans to school that day, because I am going to win the ribbon for my human, Fred Barkley."

I couldn't help it. The hair on the back of my neck stood straight up. Sure, the walls of Fred's office were lined with ribbons Sweetcakes had won at other competitions, but if any dog deserved to win the ribbon during our Open House, it was me. After all, I am a Wonder Dog. Not only that, but I had to help Maggie forget about mean Miss Frimple.

I was getting ready to tell Sweetcakes that, really I was. But Sweetcakes and Clyde turned away and walked to the back corner of the yard before I had the chance.

"Can you believe that dog?" I finally blurted.

Blondie batted her eyes at me. "Of

course not," she said. "After all, my hair is the fluffiest, and my human is ever so nice. If any dog deserves to win a ribbon for her human, it's me."

I stared at Blondie. True, she sure was beautiful. But could she beat *me*? Then Casanova, the Chihuahua, spoke up. He had a little voice, but we heard it loud and clear.

"My human always lets me ride in her purse and takes me shopping," he said.

"She deserves that blue ribbon more than anyone."

"No way, shorty," Rhett, the Irish setter, interrupted. "Scarlett and I can run through the tunnels the fastest. We'll win, no doubt about it!"

Suddenly, all the dogs within hearing distance were arguing. Every dog, that is, except Woodrow. And Petey, of course. He was too busy digging.

I couldn't believe it. Not a single dog had noticed that they had a Wonder Dog in their midst. Me. I deserved to win that contest.

Woodrow stood up and waddled into the middle of the pack. "Quiet!" he howled.

Immediately, we stopped yapping and looked at Woodrow. When Woodrow spoke, we listened.

"Not everyone can win," he said. "Whenever there's a contest, that means

there is only one winner. That doesn't mean you can't have fun. Just remember, it's not whether you win or lose, but how you play the game."

Blondie nodded. "Woodrow is right," she said.

Floyd put down the ball in his mouth to bark in agreement.

Bubba, the pup, hopped up to Woodrow. "I don't care if I win or lose," Bubba said. "I just want to have fun."

It looked like Woodrow had saved the day. I was glad of that. Now the rest of the dogs wouldn't be so disappointed when I won that blue ribbon for Maggie. I smiled at the thought. My smile didn't last too long.

Sweetcakes had been listening the entire time.

"It's about time you mutts listened to reason," she growled, "because there's no way you can beat me." And then

Sweetcakes took a step in my direction. "Especially Jack. Jack has about as much chance of winning the agility competition as a turtle has of becoming president!"

WOODROW'S PLAN

Before Sweetcakes could take another step, Petey darted between us and started digging. Obviously, Petey didn't have a clue about what was happening.

"Out of my way," Sweetcakes growled.

Sweetcakes hopped over Petey. "That pup is more pesky than a fleet of fleas," she said with a sneer.

"Yeah, yeah," Clyde said. "Fleet of fleas."

"Sweetcakes knows I am the only other dog in the yard that could win the agility competition," I said as soon as they were gone. "I'm not going to let Sweetcakes scare me. I'm going to make Maggie happy by winning that blue ribbon."

Woodrow scratched one of his long ears. "Does it really take winning a ribbon to make your human happy?" he asked.

Floyd shook his head all the way down to his tail. "My human never expects me to win anything," he told his pals. "He just likes to play ball with me."

I sat down and scratched my head. "I have to win," I told my friends. "I'd do anything for Maggie."

Blondie nudged my shoulder. I knew Blondie would understand. "Every one of us would do anything for our humans," she said. "The agility contest would be the perfect time, especially since our humans will be there on the day of the competition—every dog's human except one: Petey's."

"Poor Petey," Floyd said. "His human is out of town."

We all stopped to watch Petey. He was still digging in the same spot. His little legs worked overtime. Of course, all he accomplished was making empty holes.

Just then, a big hairy cat hopped on top of the wall. It was the one and only Tazz. Miss Frimple's cat had a bad habit of showing up at the worst times. This was no exception.

"So, I hear there's a contest," she purred.

"What do *you* know about it?" I barked.

"Just that a cat would be a sure winner." With that she began to strut along the brick wall.

Petey caught sight of Tazz and yipped. He raced after Tazz as if she were a sirloin steak. Of course, Tazz was safely out of reach, and Petey had no chance of catching her. Tazz swished her tail in the air and pranced along the top of the wall.

That just made Petey more determined to catch her. He yipped again and raced over the agility equipment so fast he was a blur. He darted through a tunnel, dashed across the balance beam, and ran up and over the seesaw. No matter how hard he tried, Petey couldn't get near Tazz's tail, and Tazz knew it.

"Petey's energetic, that's for sure," I pointed out.

"And fast," Floyd added. "Very fast."

Suddenly, Woodrow sat up straighter than I'd ever seen him. "And very good. Petey could be a real agility champion. He must be in shape because of all the digging he does. I think he has the best chance of beating Sweetcakes," Woodrow observed. "If only we could get him to stop digging long enough to teach him the right way to race over the agility course."

"I bet winning the contest would help Petey not miss his human so much," Bubba said.

Floyd stopped chewing on his toy long enough to nod. "I bet his human would be surprised to come back to town and find his pup wearing a blue ribbon!"

Blondie's eyes lit up. "Woodrow's plan is perfect! We all have to help Petey win!"

WINNER

I couldn't believe my Wonder Dog ears. First, Sweetcakes was against me. Now even my best friends were thinking of another winner. What was a Wonder Dog to do?

My friends were too busy planning how they could help Petey win the contest to notice when I walked away. I searched the yard. There was a shady spot under a tree. It was the perfect place for me to curl up and think things over.

I circled three times and plopped

down, my back to my friends and my nose pressed up to the brick wall surrounding Barkley's School for Dogs. I was ready for a long, lonely nap.

It was not to be.

"What's wrong, Poochie?" a high voice murmured.

I knew that voice.

I opened one eye and peered up at the wall. Sure enough, there sat Tazz, her long, black-and-gold tail slowly swishing just out of snapping distance.

I closed my eyes and pretended I hadn't seen her.

"It looks like Jack the Wonder Dog has the blue-ribbon blues," she meowed.

I tried to cover my ears with my paws. I wanted to hide.

Tazz may be sassy, but she must have noticed that my tail was hanging a bit lower than usual. "What's the matter?" she asked. "Cat got your tongue?"

"There's going to be a contest," I blurted. "I want to win it for Maggie, but everyone is plotting against me."

"Everyone?" Tazz purred. "Even your friends?"

I sighed. "Even my friends," I said. "They want to help Petey win because they think he has the best chance."

Tazz stood up and stretched, her back making a perfect arch. Then she sat down and curled her tail around her paws.

"I want to win that contest," I said. "And make Maggie happy."

"You're right," Tazz purred.

The hair on my back smoothed out a bit when she said that. "Of course I'm right," I said.

Tazz nodded and preened her paw. "Maggie would be happy. But other things make humans happy, too."

Tazz was trying to give me advice, which I figured was about as useful as a

spinach-flavored chew toy. I didn't want to listen, but Tazz kept talking in that irritating meow of hers.

"The way I see it," Tazz purred, "there's more than one way to be a winner. What kind of winner do you want to be, Jack?"

I sat up. Could it be that Tazz was right?

I thought it over and knew right away.

"The kind that wears a blue ribbon!" I barked.

MY CHOICE

I grinned. Not just any doggie grin. I grinned from one slightly yellowed back tooth to another. I pushed out my chest and nodded. I was going to win.

You've heard of humans working their tails off—well, that's just about what I did that next week. I put my Wonder Dog heart into training. At first, I tried leaping over the bars. I didn't have a lot of luck.

Whack! My paw hit the bar as I jumped over. Let me tell you, it didn't feel good.

"Are you all right?" Blondie asked me.

I nodded, trying not to let Blondie know that my paw felt pretty sore.

"You know," Blondie said, "Petey could use your help on the seesaw." I looked over at the seesaw. Floyd and Woodrow were coaching Petey on the right moves. It looked like Petey was doing fine.

"Sorry," I told Bondie. "I don't have time to help Petey. I have to practice, myself."

Blondie sighed. "Okay," she said. "Good

luck." Blondie trotted off to help Petey. I looked at her fluffy white tail, and all I could think was *traitor*. Why wasn't anyone helping me?

"Jack," Bubba said, like a true friend. "Try the tunnels." I trotted over and sailed through the tunnels like a rabbit down a hole.

"That's pretty good," Bubba nodded, "but it's not as fast as Sweetcakes or Petey."

Bubba was only a puppy, so I didn't take him seriously.

When I finally collapsed on the ground after practice, Floyd was waiting for me.

"Hi, Floyd," I said, panting from all my hard work.

Floyd looked up from his favorite chew toy. "I'm worried about you, Jack," Floyd said. His brown beagle eyes told me he was telling the truth.

"Don't worry about me," I bragged.

"I've been practicing hard. I'm sure to win."

"It's just that you're being so competitive," Floyd said. "You aren't around much," he continued. "We miss you."

I hung my head. Sure, I felt bad, but I was mad, too. Why couldn't anyone understand how much winning meant to me?

"I can't help it," I explained to Floyd. "I have to practice if I'm going to win, and I can't let anyone get in my way."

Floyd pushed his chew toy away. I gulped. Obviously, Floyd was upset. He had nearly chewed through his favorite toy.

"You're acting just like Sweetcakes," Floyd said. "You don't care about anything except winning."

I stared hard at Floyd. I wasn't like Sweetcakes. Was I?

THiS iS iT

I practically danced down the street on the day of competition, pulling hard on my leash. I couldn't wait to get to school. Maggie would be so proud when I beat the other dogs out of the blue ribbon.

"This is it," Maggie told me when we reached the doorstep. "Let's go have fun."

I pulled Maggie around a whole group of humans and dogs in the waiting room. I didn't take time to sniff any of the shoes.

I only nodded to Floyd and the scruffy

loafers his human wore. I didn't even stop to talk to Blondie and her human in shiny high heels. I was in such a hurry to get to the start of the competition I barely noticed Woodrow and his human in leather shoes. My friends were excited to be with their humans, but I had no time to chat.

"Whoa," Fred Barkley said when I pulled Maggie up to him. "Where's the fire?"

I sniffed. If there was a fire anywhere around, my Wonder Dog nose could sniff it out in no time flat. I smelled nothing except for lots of humans wearing perfume and the regular Barkley doggie scents.

Maggie laughed. "No fire. Jack just couldn't wait to get here for the competition."

"Why don't we let him go first, then?" Fred asked.

My heart thumped so loudly, I figured every dog would start barking at the noise. Instead, they gathered around Fred outside as he announced the start of the competition.

Fred blew the whistle and I took off. I sailed over one bar and under another. I raced through the tunnels. I felt like a king when Maggie yelled, "Go, Jack!" I was doing great until I hit the seesaw. And I do

mean *hit.* I smacked my nose right on the end of the board.

To my surprise, Blondie barked for me. "That's okay, Jack. You're still doing great."

Her words helped me to finish, but I hung my head down as several other dogs competed. I admit it. I felt miserable. How could I win a ribbon for hitting my nose?

"Go, Sweetcakes," Fred cheered. I snapped my head up. Sweetcakes turned and looked at me before starting the course.

"This is how it's done," Sweetcakes growled at me. I gulped and watched. All the humans clapped when Sweetcakes did a perfect jump. They clapped a lot. Even Maggie.

My tail drooped lower and lower as Sweetcakes ran across the seesaw without missing a single step.

When Sweetcakes crossed the finish line, she held her head higher than ever. Fred Barkley patted Sweetcakes on the head and said the word we were all thinking. "Perfect."

PETEY

I sulked away from Maggie and hid behind the shed. Maggie probably didn't want to have anything to do with a loser like me. Someone else was hiding behind the shed, too, because I heard crying.

"Petey?" I said. "Is that you?"

The little brown-and-white ball of fur uncurled and looked up at me. "Hi, Jack," Petey whimpered.

"What's wrong?" I asked.

Petey hung his head. "I don't think I can do it," Petey admitted. "What if I fall off the balance beam? What if I knock over the bars or hit my nose on the seesaw?"

Obviously, Petey hadn't seen me hit my nose, but I didn't mention that. I tried to cheer him up, as any Wonder Dog would.

"If any of those things happen," I told Petey softly, "you just keep going and have fun. Remember what Woodrow said?"

"What?" Petey said, sniffling.

"It's not whether you win or lose, it's . . ."

". . . how you play the game," Blondie said coming up behind me. Blondie smiled at me and I smiled back. It's funny, but Blondie liked me even though I wouldn't win. I felt bad that I had been such a terrible sport, but Petey still had a chance.

"You can win this competition," I told Petey. "I know you can." I had never been surer of anything.

"I don't care about winning," Petey whimpered. "Besides, my human isn't here to cheer me on."

Blondie nudged Petey. "We'll cheer for you," she said, "and so will our humans."

"Okay," Petey said with a gulp. "I'll do it. Thanks." Petey dashed out to the starting line just as Fred called his name. When Fred blew the whistle, Petey was a blur.

"Go, Petey!" Floyd and Woodrow barked. All the other dogs, except for Sweetcakes and Clyde, cheered, too.

"Howl-a-riffic," I barked to Blondie. "He's dog-awesome."

Blondie nodded. "We told you he could win."

I nodded and raced over to Maggie. I barked when Petey sailed over bar after bar. For a little dog, he really could jump.

Maggie saw me barking, and she cheered, too. All the humans clapped and cheered for the little dog who tried so hard.

Harry the Westie yipped, and a Dalmatian named Dottie even barked extra loud. But then under all the cheering, barking, and clapping I heard something that wasn't quite so friendly. In fact, it sounded downright mean. It was Sweetcakes, and she was growling at Petey.

SOMETHING HORRIBLE

Growling wasn't all that Sweetcakes was doing. She crept slowly on the ground behind some bushes. Right behind her crawled Clyde. I looked around. Everyone else's eyes focused on Petey, except for one other hound's.

Woodrow nudged up beside me. Over the sound of barking and clapping he asked, "What is Sweetcakes up to?"

I shrugged, and then a terrible idea came over me. Sweetcakes had it out for Petey. I knew Sweetcakes wanted to win

no matter what, but would she do something so horrible? I nodded. She would.

"Sweetcakes is trying to keep Petey from winning," I told Woodrow. I didn't bother whispering because everyone was clapping and cheering for Petey as he zipped through a tunnel. He had two more tunnels and then the seesaw. If he did those perfectly, he would be a sure winner.

I scratched my ear. Poor Petey. He didn't do anything halfway. He was really trying hard. I wanted Petey to do his best. I still didn't want to lose, but I certainly didn't want to hurt Petey. Floyd was wrong. I wasn't like Sweetcakes at all.

Cold chills ran down my tail when I realized what Sweetcakes had in mind. She was under the seesaw and she was digging. If someone didn't stop her fast, the seesaw would be lopsided and Petey would surely fall. I stood up straight. My

Wonder Dog senses kicked into high gear.

"I've got to help Petey," I told Woodrow before slinking off around the bushes. I crawled through the dirt on my belly and caught up with Clyde.

"Hey, Clyde," I whispered. "There are treats by the back door." That's all Clyde needed to hear. He dashed off as if a ghost were on his tail. I knew Sweetcakes wouldn't be so easy, but I had to try.

"Sweetcakes," I barked. "Stop that."

Sweetcakes turned from her digging to look at me. "Who's going to make me?" she asked.

I gulped and said the only thing I could. "Me, Jack, the Wonder Dog."

Sweetcakes laughed. "Isn't that Jack, the Underwear Dog?"

My ears turned red, but I couldn't let Sweetcakes know that it bothered me. I had to keep her from digging. "You don't want to win this way," I told her, stalling

for time. "Cheating is not the answer."

"Whatever works," Sweetcakes snarled at me. "If it weren't for this punk pup, Petey, I would be the sure winner."

"No, you're cheating," I said to Sweetcakes. "And I'll tell everyone."

Sweetcakes started to dig again. "No one will believe you," she snapped.

"All they have to do is look at your dirty paws to know you did the digging," I barked.

Sweetcakes swirled her body around and growled. Then an evil smile filled her face. "Look at your paws, Jack. Everyone knows how much you wanted to win. I'll tell them you did it."

I stared in disbelief at my paws. They were dusty from crawling through the dirt. My heart slid all the way down into my tail. Sweetcakes was right. Everyone would believe Sweetcakes's evil lie, and Petey would still get hurt.

As Sweetcakes turned back around to dig, a hundred ideas raced through my mind. I didn't have time to do any of them, though. Petey was entering the homestretch. So I did the only thing I could.

I closed my eyes and clamped my jaws down as hard as I could on Sweetcakes's stubby tail.

10

BLUE-RiBBon TiME

Petey zipped over the seesaw. Luckily, he didn't look down or he would have seen a snarling Doberman pinscher with a Wonder Dog stuck on her tail. It wasn't a pretty sight, but it worked.

The minute Petey finished, I let go of Sweetcakes's tail and ran to Maggie's side. I stuck to Maggie like a flea on a wet dog. Surely, Sweetcakes wouldn't attack me in front of people. Or would she?

"And now it's time for the prizes," Fred Barkley announced from a small stage. He opened a box full of glittering ribbons. "Woodrow," Fred announced, "for you we have the Calmest Dog award." Everyone clapped as Woodrow's owner pinned a yellow ribbon to Woodrow's collar. Woodrow smiled and gave a little nod.

"The award for Best-Groomed Dog goes to Blondie," Fred announced.

"Way to go, Blondie," I barked as Blondie's owner pinned a pink ribbon on her diamond-studded collar. Blondie batted her long eyelashes at me and grinned.

Fred handed out ribbon after ribbon. Floyd got one for Best Retriever, and Rhett and Scarlett received ribbons for being the best jumpers. I tried to keep one eye on Sweetcakes to see if she was coming after me, so when they called my name I was shocked. I looked up at Maggie.

"Jack, you won a ribbon," Maggie said.

Me? Jack, the Wonder Dog, had won a ribbon?

"Jack," Fred said. "Come and get your ribbon for Most-Improved Dog."

Let me tell you, I danced up onto that stage. I could hardly stand still while Maggie pinned the purple ribbon to my collar. Purple was Maggie's favorite color. My friends cheered. It was a moment I'll never forget.

"Oh, Jack," Maggie said, giving me a hug after we were off the stage. "I'm so proud of you." I knew then that ribbons

weren't what mattered. The love of friends and a good human meant more to me than anything.

"And now," Fred Barkley announced. "It's time for the Blue Ribbon."

Everyone clapped and held their breaths. "This year there are two winners," Fred continued.

Two winners? I thought.

"Yes," Fred said. "It's never happened before, but this year there is a tie. The first blue-ribbon winner is Sweetcakes!"

Everyone clapped, or cheered, or barked at the same time. Sweetcakes raced onto the stage, and Fred pinned a big blue ribbon to her collar. Sweetcakes sneered at me, and I knew that she hadn't forgotten about my biting her tail.

"And the other Blue Ribbon winner is Petey!" Fred announced.

Petey stood all alone to the side of the crowd. He didn't know what to do. He

didn't have an owner to pin the ribbon on his collar. I looked at Petey and then at Maggie. I whined and Maggie smiled. Have I ever mentioned how smart Maggie is? She knew just what to do.

Maggie left me to walk Petey onto the stage. Everyone clapped or barked as Maggie pinned a big blue ribbon on Petey's collar.

Blondie nudged me on the shoulder.

"I'm proud of you, Jack," she said.

I shook my head and grinned. "You were right all along. Winning isn't about ribbons at all," I told her. "It's about friendship. And thanks to all my friends at Barkley's School for Dogs, I am the biggest winner of all!"

ABOUT THE AUTHORS

Marcia Thornton Jones and Debbie Dadey used to work together at the same elementary school—Marcia taught in the classroom and Debbie was a librarian. But now they love writing about a totally different kind of school . . . where the students have four legs and a tail!

Marcia lives in Lexington, Kentucky, and Debbie lives in Fort Collins, Colorado. Their own pets have inspired them to write about Jack and his friends at Barkley's School. These authors have also written The Adventures of the Bailey School Kids, The Bailey City Monsters, and the Triplet Trouble series together.

Fetch all the books in this doggone cool series!

AVAiLABLE iN BOOKSTORES NOW!